NEXT DOOR'S DOG HAS A JOB

NEXT DOOR'S DOG HAS A JOB

GINA DAWSON

ILLUSTRATED BY VIVIENNE DA SILVA

NEW
HOLLAND

Tom sees Pepper at the gate. Pepper has her ball and is wagging her tail. She is always happy to see Tom come home from school because that means cuddles, a walk and sometimes a ball game.

Dad is on the footpath, talking with Kate. Kate's dog Bailey is there too. Bailey and Kate are always together, and when they go out Bailey wears a bright yellow jacket.

Kate waves goodbye. Dad gives Tom a hug. "Let's put Pepper inside," he says. "We're going to the supermarket."

In the kitchen, Tom has a glass of milk. As he drinks he has an idea.

"Can we buy Pepper a yellow jacket so that she can come to the supermarket too?" asks Tom.

"No," says Dad. "Pepper can't have a jacket like Bailey's. Bailey is a working dog and he wears the jacket when he is doing his job."

"What's Bailey's job?" Tom asks.

"Bailey looks after Kate because Kate isn't well," explains Dad.

"But, Kate doesn't look sick," Tom grumbles. He wants Pepper to come to the supermarket. "She looks healthy, just like us."

"You can't always know if people are healthy or sick by looking at them, Tom," Dad replies quietly. "Kate has an illness that no one can see and if she didn't have Bailey she wouldn't go out at all."

Tom thinks for a moment.

"How did Bailey learn to look after Kate?" he asks.

"First Bailey learned the same things that Pepper learned, like how to come when he is called, and to sit and stay," says Dad. "Then Bailey did extra lessons for a long time."

"Like what," asks Tom, still sounding grumpy.
"What can Bailey do that Pepper can't?"

"Well," says Dad. "Bailey knows how to use the stairs and a lift, ride on
the bus, go to the mall and stay close to Kate everywhere she goes."

"He makes sure Kate gets up when her alarm goes off in the morning and catches the bus for work on time. Bailey knows lots of other things too," Dad continues.

"Bailey has passed a special test. He has a card with his photo on it, which Kate carries in her purse. That means Bailey is allowed to go everywhere with Kate, even to work."

"Wow!" says Tom, sounding happier. "Bailey must be really clever and love Kate to look after her so well!"

"Yes, and Kate loves Bailey too," says Dad. "They look after each other."

"Can Bailey play ball and go for walks, like Pepper does?" asks Tom.

"Yes," answers Dad. "When Bailey is at home he relaxes and has fun.
When he goes out he wears his jacket so that people know he is working."

Tom cuddles Pepper, looking thoughtful.

"Come on," says Dad. "We need to get to the supermarket."

At the supermarket, Tom pushes the trolley while Dad shops. Suddenly Tom gets excited.

"Look, Dad!" he calls. "There's Kate and Bailey now. I'm going to go and say hello and give Bailey a hug. I want to tell him what a clever dog he is."

"Wait!" says Dad quickly. "Bailey is wearing his jacket. He is working and you must never, ever distract a working dog by patting or talking to them. Do you understand why, Tom?"

Tom thinks for a moment.

"I think so," he says. "It's like when I interrupt you when you are working and you forget what you were doing because you can't think about two things at once."

"Good boy," says Dad, smiling. "That's exactly right. If Bailey is looking at you, he can't be concentrating on Kate."

Kate waves from the end of the aisle and disappears around the corner.

Dad and Tom finish the shopping and load it into the car.

"Dad," Tom asks. "I've seen dogs in jackets before but they were big dogs and yellow or black. Bailey is brown and white and he is small! How can he be a real helper dog?"

Dad thinks for a moment. "Tom, helper dogs, or Service Dogs, which is what they are called, can be little or big, and any shape and color. They are trained to do many important jobs.

"A person may not be able to hear or see or fetch things for themselves. Or perhaps, like Kate, they have a different illness that the dog helps with," Dad says.

"Okay," says Tom, putting on his seatbelt. "I guess Pepper won't ever get to be a Service Dog then."

Dad smiles.

"Everyone in our family is healthy and happy, and we can look after ourselves and each other without any help," he says.

"So we are very, very lucky! Now, let's go home and unpack the shopping and then take Pepper to the park for a ball game before it gets too late."

NOTE TO PARENTS, CAREGIVERS AND EDUCATORS

Service Dogs are highly trained dogs that assist their human companions in a number of ways. These include, but are not limited to, providing assistance to those with vision, hearing and mobility impairments, epilepsy, autism and mental health conditions including Post Traumatic Stress Disorder and anxiety.

The times when only Labradors and Retrievers were trained for this role have long passed, and many breeds are now used.

Most of us are aware of teaching children to be "dog smart" and not approach unknown dogs in any situation. However the novelty of seeing a dog in a supermarket, restaurant or other public place where that may not be the norm can be a fascinating attraction to a young child.

Children should be aware of the physical or emotional difficulty that may be imposed on the dog's handler when the dog is distracted.

Discuss with the child the importance of the work these dogs perform as a team with their human companions. Emphasize that the relationship between dog and handler is a two way one, and that the dog is not just doing a job but is a highly valued, much loved and well cared for family member.

A final thought – many people with disabilities, especially "invisible" ones, do not wish to be constantly explaining why they have a Service Dog. This information is "private".

Give them and their dogs the space and opportunity to live life to their fullest.

GINA DAWSON

Author Gina Dawson spent much of her teaching career presenting a range of programs on growth and social issues in schools. She is a lifelong lover of dogs, an experienced trainer and is cognizant of the disability sector. *Next Door's Dog Has A Job* was written as a result of observations as to how children may inadvertently cause difficulties or stress to dog-and-person teams that they encounter. It aims to promote discussion and understanding about the important role Service Dogs play within society, the range of disabilities they assist with and the work they do.

VIVIENNE DA SILVA

Illustrator Vivienne da Silva has been drawing ever since she was old enough to hold a pencil. Inspired by countless animated films as a child, she scoured her local library for books on how to draw, and this ignited what became a lifelong passion. She still adores animated movies today, as well as dogs, tea, musicals and terrible puns.

Next Door's Dog Has a Job is her first illustrated book.

Dedicated to Kiera, the amazing little dark one.

And to Blackie, Sandy, Sultan, Sheba, Heidi, Barney and Christie.
All so special in your own way. Loved and remembered always.

First published in 2018 by New Holland Publishers
London • Sydney • Auckland

131-151 Great Titchfield Street, London WIW 5BB, United Kingdom
1/66 Gibbes Street, Chatswood, NSW 2067, Australia
5/39 Woodside Ave, Northcote, Auckland 0627, New Zealand

newhollandpublishers.com

A record of this book is held at the British Library and the National Library of Australia.

ISBN 9781921024870

Group Managing Director: Fiona Schultz
Publisher: Monique Butterworth
Project Editor: Kaitlyn Smith
Designer: Catherine Meachen
Production Director: James Mills-Hicks
Printer: Toppan Leefung Printing

10 9 8 7 6 5 4 3 2 1

Keep up with New Holland Publishers on Facebook
facebook.com/NewHollandPublishers